Yoon
and the
Jade
Bracelet

Helen Recorvits

Pictures by Gabi Swiatkowska

Frances Foster Books

Farrar, Straus and Giroux

New York

My name is Yoon. I came here from Korea, a country far away.

Soon after we settled in America, it was time to celebrate my birthday. I was hoping for a very special present—a jump rope. I watched the girls in my school yard turning such a rope and jumping and singing happy songs. I wanted so much to jump and sing with them, but I was still the new girl. I had not been invited yet.

On my birthday, my mother called to me. "Little Yoon, come! I have a present for you!"

I clapped my hands and ran to her.

She handed me something thin and flat wrapped in pretty paper. "Happy birthday!" she said.

Jump ropes are not thin and flat, I thought. I tried not to show my disappointment. "Thank you, Mother," I said, smiling.

My mother watched excitedly as I opened the present. It was a Korean
storybook about a little girl who was tricked by a tiger. I knew the story, and I
laughed at the silly girl.

"The pictures are colorful," I said.

"Yes, they remind me of the pictures you draw, Yoon."

I liked the book, but my heart still longed for a jump rope.

"And here is another surprise," my mother said as she handed me a lovely box.

Inside was a pale green bracelet. I held its cool smoothness in my hand.

"A jade bracelet, Yoon," my mother said. "When I was a young girl, my own mother gave me this very bracelet. Now I am giving it to you."

"It is a wonderful present," I said. It was so wonderful I felt afraid to take it from her.

"Look, Yoon," she said. "Here is your Korean name now etched inside." She showed me the dancing symbols that meant Shining Wisdom.

Then she told me the story of jade. "Jade is a stone from the earth, but it is called the gem of the heavens. Green is the color of happiness and hope, and it is said that wearing jade will bring you good luck. It is the symbol of truth and friendship. A precious gem for a precious daughter." My mother slipped the bracelet onto my wrist.

At lunchtime the next day at school, I sat at the end of the table. An older girl from another class sat down beside me.

"Oh, look," she said, "you are wearing such a pretty bracelet!"

"Thank you," I said.

"You are alone today. I will be your friend. Would you like to play jump rope with me?" the older girl asked.

Jump rope? "Yes, yes!" I answered.

"Good! I will teach you. We will have fun!"

"Yes!" I said, smiling at my new friend. Jump rope!

After lunch we ran outside to play awhile. The older girl tied one end of the rope to the fence. Then she gave me the other end to turn, turn. She jumped and sang while I turned faster, slower, faster. I turned and turned. My arm grew tired. I had learned the rope part very well, but I really wanted to learn the jump part.

"When will *I* jump?" I asked.

"Tomorrow," the older girl said. The bell rang. It was time to go inside, and she took the rope from me.

"I really like your bracelet," she said. "In America friends share things. If we are going to be friends, you should share your bracelet with me. You should let me wear it—just for today."

My birthday bracelet? Oh, no, no, no. I could not share that. My mother's own mother had given it to her, and now it was mine. No, no, I shook my head.

"Well . . . then how can we be friends?" the older girl asked. "I thought you wanted to learn how to jump rope?"

I slipped the jade bracelet off and held it in my hand. My mother said it would bring me good luck and good friends. But sharing it did not seem right.

Quickly the older girl grabbed the bracelet from me and twisted it onto her own wrist. "Do not worry," she said. "I will give it back tomorrow."

When I got home from school, I went straight to my room. My mother came in to check on me. As I sat on my bed reading my new Korean storybook, she reached for my arm and gasped.

"Where is your bracelet, Yoon?"

I shrugged with shame, not trusting myself to speak.

"Oh, I see a sad face. Did you lose it at school, Yoon?"

I shrugged again.

"Maybe it rolled away and is hiding somewhere here," she said with teary eyes. And she kneeled to look under my bed.

"Mother," I said, tugging her sleeve, "I left it at school. I will get it tomorrow."

The next morning I waited in the school yard for the older girl. She was still wearing my jade bracelet.

"It is time to give back my bracelet," I said.

"I will give it to you later," she said, rushing past me.

All morning my heart was heavy with worry. I could not remember how to spell "cat" or how to add two plus two.

After lunch, when the children ran outside, I found the older girl again. "You have my bracelet and I want it back," I said.

"Stop bothering me! Do not be a pest!" She pushed me away and laughed.

I was just like the silly girl in my storybook. I had been tricked by a tiger.

Back in my classroom, I laid my head on my desk.

"What is wrong, Yoon?" my teacher asked.

I told my teacher about the older girl, and she sent for her.

"Do you have something that belongs to Yoon?" my teacher asked her. "Is that her bracelet you are wearing?"

"Oh, no!" the older girl said with her trickster tongue. "It is mine!"

"No! It is my birthday bracelet!" I said.

The children in my class gathered around us.

"Yoon was wearing it yesterday," the ponytail girl said.

"Yes," said the freckle boy. "I saw it, too."

"Can you tell me something about this bracelet, Yoon?" my teacher asked.

"My mother gave it to me," I answered, looking into the tiger girl's face. "This bracelet is a symbol of kindness and courage. It is a symbol of jade friendship—true friendship."

"Now *you* tell me about this bracelet," my teacher said to the older girl.

"Well . . . it is smooth and green," she answered in a sure voice.

I worried I would never get my bracelet back. I did not feel like Shining Wisdom. My mother should have named me Shining Fool instead.

Then I had a very good idea. I whispered something into my teacher's ear.

"So tell me about the inside of this bracelet," she asked the older girl.

"Well . . . it is smooth and green," she repeated.

The teacher told her to take it off, and the girl struggled to get it over her hand. My teacher looked inside and saw the dancing Korean symbols.

"Do you know what this says?" she asked the girl.

"No," the older girl said. "Well . . . I thought it was my bracelet. I used to have one just like it. Maybe this one does belong to Yoon."

My teacher's eyes said Older-girl-you-are-in-trouble.

Then my teacher slid the jade bracelet easily over my hand. "Here is your name bracelet, Shining Wisdom."

And it fit. Perfectly.

My mother saw the bracelet on my wrist after school. She clapped her hands. "Aha! It *was* at school!"

"Mother," I asked, "does wearing jade make wishes come true?"

"Yes," she said. "It is known to happen." She smiled. "And what are your wishes?"

So I told her about my jump rope wish and my wish for true friends.

And I told her a story about a wise girl who tricked a tiger.

To my jade-true friend Frances Foster
—H.R.
For Z̊ak, she knows why
—G.S.

Text copyright © 2008 by Helen Recorvits
Pictures copyright © 2008 by Gabi Swiatkowska
All rights reserved
Distributed in Canada by Douglas & McIntyre Ltd.
Color separations by Chroma Graphics PTE Ltd.
Printed and bound in China by South China Printing Co. Ltd.
Designed by Jay Colvin
First edition, 2008
1 3 5 7 9 10 8 6 4 2

www.fsgkidsbooks.com

Library of Congress Cataloging-in-Publication Data
Recorvits, Helen.
    Yoon and the jade bracelet / Helen Recorvits ; pictures by Gabi
Swiatkowska.— 1st ed.
        p.   cm.
    Summary: Although she really would have liked a jump rope for her birthday,
Yoon is happy to receive a Korean picture book and a jade bracelet passed down
from her grandmother, and when she wears the bracelet to school it seems as if
her wish for a jump rope and a friend is about to come true.
    ISBN-13: 978-0-374-38689-4
    ISBN-10: 0-374-38689-7
    1. Korean Americans—Juvenile fiction.   [1. Korean Americans—Fiction.
2. Bracelets—Fiction.   3. Friendship—Fiction.   4. Bullies—Fiction.
5. Schools—Fiction.]   I. Swiatkowska, Gabriela, ill.   II. Title.

PZ7.R24435 Yja 2008
[E]—dc22
                                                                      2006048402